PERFECT NO MATTER WHAT

WARDHAM BOOK 7

ZOE YORK

ZOYO PRESS

COPYRIGHT

Copyright © 2014, 2016 Zoe York
All rights reserved.

PERFECT NO MATTER WHAT

DEDICATION

be happy, just the way you are
be loved, just the way you are

For my Romance Diva friends in the Love Is… anthology, for whom I wrote this story.

ABOUT THIS BOOK

Perfect No Matter What is a short story sequel to *What Once Was Perfect*. It takes place after *When They Weren't Looking*, Laney's sister's book, and contains spoilers for that story. Go and read that book first if you haven't yet!

They keep meaning to say I do…

Laney and Kyle lost each other once. Now they've found a way back together, and nothing will break them apart. But real life—two busy careers, nosy family members, and very different priorities for their oft-discussed yet still hypothetical wedding—keeps them from formalizing the forever they promised each other more than a year ago.

A business trip for Kyle and a last-minute rearranging of Laney's schedule provides the perfect fantasy escape to re-focus on what really matters.

WARNING: This story starts with a blow-job and just gets dirtier from there. Because who ever said that filthy sex and sweet wedding vows weren't compatible?

1
____

As he had been all too often lately, Kyle woke to the quiet hum of something vibrating in his fiancée's hand. He stiffened before he could control his reaction. It wasn't her fault. He needed to be more understanding, but this ruined their plans for the day.

"You're mad." Even through her sleepy slur, he could hear the sadness in Laney's voice.

He tugged her close, relishing the soft dip and swell of her waist and hip under his palm. "No, just disappointed."

She rolled on top of him, still holding her offending pager. "It's this resident, he's super needy. I'm going to call, talk him through the consult, and then I'll come back to bed for an hour. I'll need to go in for rounds, but I promise we'll make it to the market today."

"I'm awake. You don't need to go to the den to call him." Kyle kissed Laney's neck and squeezed her bottom. As if on cue, Buddy scrambled off his ridiculous dog bone pillow bed in the corner and started nosing Kyle's foot. "Be right back."

Four in the morning. *Jesus.* He thought waking before dawn on a regular basis would be a thing of the past when he moved off the family farm. He had to go and fall in love with a surgeon. And get a dog. His little family. He loved them both, even if they interfered with a good sleep-in.

He followed Buddy down the stairs and across the kitchen to the back slider. While the black and white mutt did his business in their small fenced yard, Kyle put coffee on and refilled the stainless steel water and kibble bowls next to the fridge.

A scratch at the door told him his butler services were required again. Then he got a lick on the leg on the way past and the early morning business was forgiven. He grabbed a banana and left Buddy downstairs, closing the gate at the kitchen door for good measure. He had an hour with his woman. He planned to make the most of it.

Laney lay on the bed, phone pressed to her ear and head tossed back in frustration. Kyle quietly stripped out of his shorts and rejoined her on the bed, pressing his erection into the naked hip peeking out from beneath the hem of his college swim team shirt. Now threadbare in spots, the shirt was still her favourite sleeping garment. She'd worn it in college, the first time they fell in love, and when they broke up he'd put it away. More than a decade later, he'd given it to her again and this time there would be no pause to their relationship. Too many years had passed, but hindsight was twenty-twenty.

Now they were living in the moment, together, and he couldn't be happier. Except for the working around the clock thing, but that was part of the deal of loving Laney.

She hung up the phone and turned into his embrace. "I need to leave in forty-seven minutes."

"Then I'll make you scream for thirty and we can rush through a shower."

———

LANEY DIDN'T GET out of the hospital until almost noon, but they made it to the farmer's market. A simple bit of togetherness was all Kyle had asked for and no matter how busy she got, she wanted to give that to him.

They stopped at the Italian deli for olives and *coppa*, then the veggie stand across the way for cucumbers, tomatoes and basil. Laney grabbed a second cucumber and Kyle wrapped his arm around her waist, tugging her tight to his side.

"Is that all you're going to eat while I'm gone?" He laughed against her hair as he nuzzled closer.

"Well, this and a daily pick-up of Thai food, yes." She looped her arms around his neck. "You're only going to be away for five days. I'll survive."

He stole her mouth for a quick kiss then patted her on

the butt. "Let's get you home and fed before my flight. Who knows when your next good meal will be."

An idea started to percolate as they made a late lunch together, Kyle making a balsamic vinaigrette while Laney chopped vegetables and a coarse baguette into similar sized cubes. She fetched a block of Pecorino cheese from the fridge and shaved thick curls onto their bowls before they dug in. "Tell me more about the conference itinerary," she prompted, waving her fork in the air.

"The first two days will be jam-packed, that's the graduate student symposium. But once the full conference gets under way, I'll probably have an afternoon or morning free each day. Willem wants to do a helicopter tour of the Grand Canyon. I think I'd just be happy checking out the Strip."

"And you're back on Thursday?"

"Yeah. The conference doesn't end until Friday, but the cheaper flight—and getting back to you—made it worthwhile."

"How much were flights on Sunday?" She thought she'd asked the question casually enough, but apparently not.

He put his fork down and reached across the table to snag her hand. "Don't."

"I'm just asking—"

"No offence, sweetheart, but you're going to get my hopes up. You won't be able to get away. And that's okay. It's not like I've had a lifelong fantasy of a dirty weekend in Vegas with you or anything." God, the things his grin did to her insides...and some important parts of her outsides, too.

"Lifelong?"

He gave her a hungry look. "Laney, you've starred in my fantasies since before I knew what made Vegas... well, Vegas."

Was she purring out loud? "We'll go sometime. I promise."

"Like we'll get away to Mexico and get married?" His doubting tone didn't hold any malice, which was a not-so-minor miracle. She really didn't deserve him and his endless patience. "Besides, we're going to New York next month for that MedEd conference." He pushed away from the table and came around to her side. He stroked the nape of her neck for a minute before gathering her hair in a ponytail and tugging her head back so he could kiss her. He pressed deeper, as if he could show her his love and promise with his passion that the details didn't matter.

Didn't matter *as much* as their love. But maybe she'd been relying on that promise and Kyle's unwavering commitment a little too much of late. Just because he understood didn't mean she couldn't surprise him.

Starting with the half hour before they had to leave for the airport. She looked up at the gorgeous man looming over her, her man, who'd let her walk away once but never would again. She slid out of her chair, dropping to her knees on the hardwood floor. A floor he'd laid with his bare hands—and a few power tools.

"Have I told you today just how much I love you?" She licked her lips as she undid his belt. Beneath the dark denim of his jeans, his solid thighs flexed toward her and he grunted his appreciation for what she was offering. "I really, really do." She dragged his zipper open, relishing the growing bulge pressing against her knuckles. She did that to him. He did everything for her, but she could bring him pleasure.

It wasn't enough, but it was something.

"We've got time if you want to go upstairs," he rasped, stroking his thumb over her lower lip. She swiped her tongue out and tasted the saltiness of his rough skin there. Different from the silky texture of his cock, still hidden behind red boxer briefs, but just as delicious. Every inch of Kyle's body made her hungry for another taste.

But she was still sore from their pre-dawn encounter. And this was just for him. She settled back on her heels and pulled her t-shirt off. She traced her fingers along the lacy edge of her bra and looked up at Kyle with her best coquettish glance. "I was thinking maybe I should jerk you off and you could come…right here."

"Jesus Christ, Laney." His normally brown eyes were darker than ink and heavy with lust. Triumphant pride roared through her body, tightening her nipples and flooding her sex. Maybe this wasn't *entirely* for him.

She wriggled closer and brushed her face against the

soft cotton triangle exposed by his open fly. Against her cheek, his erection strained for more significant contact. She twisted her head in his general direction but let her eyes drift shut, breathing in his subtle scent. Five days was nothing in the grand scheme of their relationship. Until he'd moved to Chicago, they'd done weeks at a time. But she'd gotten used to having him whenever she —or he—wanted. For love or lust or just a cuddle.

"Would you rather my mouth?" she murmured, rubbing against him like a cat in heat. "Wet and warm…I could do that thing you like with my tongue."

He made a strangled sound and fisted one hand in her hair. "Hand or mouth, Lane, I don't care which."

She grinned, not caring if she looked like the Cheshire cat, and wiggled her fingers under his waistband. He hissed in a breath, then let it out in a dirty, low laugh as she opened her mouth and took just his head inside. He'd been her first—for this and everything else —and in the decade they spent apart, she'd avoided oral sex. Now as she savoured the heavy weight of his cock on her tongue and breathed him in, she rejoiced that she'd come to love this act. And not just because, as his hands tightened in her hair, he so obviously enjoyed it.

A few tentative bobs of her head provided more than enough lubricant to take him deeper, then she did, enjoying the rough slide and reluctant retreat of his hips as he set the rhythm he wanted.

At first she just hollowed out her cheeks, sucking hard enough to keep him groaning. That sound…there was nothing better in the world than bringing him this kind of pleasure. Then she upped her game and did *the thing* with her tongue, the wiggly twist against the frenulum on the underside of the head of his cock. It started with a flutter and then grew more purposeful, teasing the stretched foreskin around his engorged and exposed crown. Side to side she twisted her head, looping her tongue around and up and back down again until he gasped. He didn't need to tap her on the shoulder and ask her what she wanted him to do—that was one of the perks of a long-term relationship, they both knew the score. If she didn't want him in her mouth, she'd move.

She didn't move. With a hum, she relaxed her jaw and let him explode on her tongue, swallowing with each pulse. Her hands had settled on his hips, and beneath her touch he was rock solid, his muscles clenched in release but also just keeping himself upright. She'd bugged him one night to tell her what his orgasms were like and she knew that right now he was hovering between pleasure and pain. She scooted out of the way and nudged him in the direction of a chair as she moved to the fridge in search of a drink.

He snagged her wrist after she poured herself a glass of iced tea, and she drank it as she sat in his lap. He stroked her back, his face buried in the crook of her arm.

"I'm going to miss you," she whispered.

"I'm going miss THAT," he teased. "And you. Is it weird that I feel like five days is a lot?"

"I had the same thought. I've gotten used to being together at some point every day."

"We'll have phone sex."

"That wasn't what I meant." She twisted to look at him more fully. He hadn't shaved, and she danced her knuckles against his stubbled jaw. "But yes, please."

2

It had taken no small amount of cajoling, bribing and out-right threatening, but by Wednesday morning Laney had cleared the rest of her week and booked Buddy into a kennel for a puppy vacation. A day of clinic on Friday had been a pain to cancel, but Kyle was worth it. Their relationship never took top priority in her life—her heart, absolutely, but never her calendar. It was time for an exception to that unfortunate rule of being a doctor. A quick call to the grad secretary in the Department of Education gave her the name of the travel agent all grant-funded travel went through, and twenty minutes later, she'd booked herself a flight to Vegas and rearranged Kyle's return flight to match hers, giving them the full weekend together in Vegas.

When he called later that day, she was on her way to O'Hare. "Hey, baby," she said over the car's built-in Bluetooth.

"On a scale of one to *hello no*, how would you feel about me going to a burlesque show?" Street noise flooded in around his voice.

Vegas was two hours behind Chicago time. "At one in the afternoon?"

He laughed. "Tonight. Willem's at the discount ticket office right now."

Shit. "How late would you be? I've got a consult after work at DermaNorth, but I was hoping we might…"

He lowered his voice. "Laney, are you asking me to give up mostly naked ladies for a totally naked you on the other end of the phone?"

She giggled. "I was planning on wearing my bunny rabbit pjs and lying to you about the naked part."

"How can I say no to that?" He raised his voice and told Willem he had other plans. She felt a momentary pang of guilt at him passing up something that sounded like a lot of fun before she remembered that she was actually on her way to see him. And she hadn't packed her bunny rabbit pjs.

A tight, nervous thrill blasted through her chest as she thought about what she HAD packed. A lot of lace, a black leather corset that she'd never in a million years wear in Chicago, and the matching ring boxes that had spent the better part of a year in her lingerie drawer. They didn't need Mexico—they had Sin City and a wide variety of twenty-four hour chapels. Guilt of a different sort reared its head as she thought of her mother and sister, both of whom would lose their minds when they found out they'd missed her wedding. Kyle's mother, too.

Tough. Kyle had wanted to elope. She'd been the one to drag her feet and worry about what others would think. Not anymore. She was all in, even if she didn't have a wedding dress. Maybe she'd get married in the corset.

"Well, we're going to find a cheap poker game for a couple of hours." Kyle cleared his throat and she jerked her attention back to the conversation. "And then you and I have a date with some dirty words after dinner."

"Counting the hours."

"Are you in the car? You sound tinny."

She bit her lip. It was highly unusual for her to have left the hospital this early. "I'm heading to the university for a meeting." Little white lies in the execution of a surprise were fine. "And baby? A burlesque show sounds fun. Not *hell no*, that's for sure. Just not tonight, okay?"

———

KYLE SWIRLED his tumbler of cheap whiskey and stacked his chips again. Willem was chewing on his bottom lip— probably some sort of tell, or fake out, but looking at the pair of jacks in his own hand and the one on the table, Kyle didn't really care. His brother, Ian, loved poker. Kyle liked numbers, but he didn't get emotionally invested. And he never read his opponents. He just played the odds.

He should have asked Laney to come with him, even if she could only get away for twenty-four hours. All week he'd seen wedding chapels advertised. Sixty bucks for a license, a few hundred for the service. Then a limo and a magnum of champagne and they'd be bonded together forever. He swallowed the last of the amber liquid in his glass. In his head, he knew it didn't matter if they were married or not. In his heart, he wanted to brand Laney as his wife.

Maybe instead of getting married he should drag her to a tattoo parlour. Stamp his name in a swirly font on her perfect ass. He pulled out his phone and texted her. **How do you feel about tattoos**?

He watched the text message turn green instead of staying blue. Damn. She was in some dark corner of the hospital without reception.

The odds of sexting preceding their phone call in a couple of hours were low. The odds of him winning this hand were pretty high, though. And when he did, he anted in for the next. Nothing to be done but have some fun.

He had his mind on a decent steak dinner, an excellent use for his winnings, when her return text came in. **For me or you?**

Maybe both. Matching ones.

What are you thinking.

Your name over my heart.

His phone rang, and he wished Willem a good time at the show. He answered as he turned to walk back to the Venetian on his own. "Be warned, Laney, I'm out in public, turning me on would be a dangerous move."

"Are you drunk?" Her laughing voice filled his ear.

"Yeah, a bit. I had a good afternoon of cards and whiskey."

"My name over your heart, eh?"

"It's already there, sweetheart, might as well make it official. Since we're never going to actually make it official."

"That's on your mind, huh?" She lowered her voice. "Is being in Vegas giving you ideas for eloping again?"

He was at the wrong end of the strip for wedding chapels, but he swung his arms out in a wide circle, narrowly missing an older couple in matching *Florida is for Lovers* t-shirts and navy blue Tilly hats. "Love is all around me, Laney, and I'm all alone."

She laughed again. "What would you do if I was there?"

"I'd toss you over my shoulder and hail a cab for the Graceland Chapel."

"You want to get married by Elvis?"

"Sounds perfect." His hotel loomed ahead of him. "Hey, listen, I'm starving. I'm going to stop at one of the restaurants before heading up to my room. Can I call you back?"

"Sure. How many restaurants are there in the Venetian?"

"I don't know. The Grand Lux is on the way to my room. Lane, this place is crazy, you gotta see it some day."

"Go eat your steak, high roller. I love you."

He had a shit-eating grin on his face as he made his way to the bar. The bartender brought him a menu, and poured him a drink, then drifted down to the other end before coming back. He stopped a few feet away. "Can I help you?"

Kyle started to answer, but the guy held up his hand. "Sorry, buddy, ladies first."

A swish of fabric and a familiar scent had him half off his stool before Laney stroked her hand down his forearm and gave him a *play along* look. "Is this seat taken?"

"All yours." He looked her up and down. Damn, she looked good. Shiny hair, bright eyes, and not a stethoscope in sight. She wore a black mini dress and strappy high heels, her legs bare and long and ever so close to his. Yes, he'd play along. "You come here often?"

"First time." She returned the admiring look and smiled a secret smile. "You in Vegas alone?"

"Sure am. My fiancée had to work."

"All work and no play?"

"I wouldn't say that."

She leaned closer and lowered her voice. "It's okay, you can tell me. What happens in Vegas…"

He closed the gap between them and brushed his mouth against her ear. "Order your drink, woman."

She grinned at the bartender and once they were alone again, she squeezed his thigh. "Miss me?"

"I missed Laney. I have no idea who this wonderful temptress is, but I think she might be trouble."

"Of the best kind, I promise."

"Dare I ask how you managed to get out here?"

A serious look drifted across her face for a moment. "It turns out, nothing's impossible if it's important enough."

"I didn't want you to feel like you had—"

"I came because I wanted to be here. With you." Sexy, teasing Laney roared back to life. "Tell me more about your fiancée."

"She's beautiful. Looks a lot like you. Has a wicked mouth."

"Not sure I can compete with that, but I'm willing to give it a go. I do this thing with my tongue…"

God, he was glad she'd made the trip. A laugh ripped up from his chest and he tossed his head back. "She has that too. She's pretty perfect."

"But she let you come to Sin City all alone. Naughty girl."

"When I get home, I should spank her." He pulled his wallet out and tossed enough on the bar for their drinks and a tip. "But since you're here, I feel like a practice paddle."

With a happy shriek, Laney let him drag her off the bar stool and they set a quick pace for the elevators.

"What about your steak?" she teased, pressing the

length of her front hard into his side. He was acutely aware of the subtle spread of her thighs, the press of her mound against his hip, and the sharp intake of breath that betrayed just how much she enjoyed the pressure right there as he ground sideways into her core.

"We'll order room service." He nipped at her ear and lowered his voice. "Maybe I'll make you my appetizer."

They held hands in the crowded elevator. Even on Kyle's floor, where the hallway was quiet, they waited until he'd opened his door before sliding together and kissing for the first time in four days. But by the time the latch clicked behind them, they were halfway naked.

Kyle picked Laney up and tossed her on the bed. He cast a quick, appreciative look at her purple lace thong before sliding it down her thighs and hitching her knees over his shoulders. He kissed his way up the inside of one thigh, dusted a breath over her gorgeous pussy, then back down the other leg, loving the way she trembled at the tease. "Do you want something, sweetheart?"

"Know any tongue tricks of your own, stranger?"

"My fiancée likes it when I do this," he said, parting her sex with two fingers. *Fuck*, he loved the scent of her. Sweet and musky. The sight of her, too. Swollen and slick with slippery desire, blond curls hiding a shiny pink secret just for him. He licked her centre, groaning in pleasure at the first taste before remembering it wasn't all about his addiction to her pussy. He owed her an orgasm. He slid one finger inside her, then another as she spread her thighs and tilted her hips in a soundless plea for more.

In tandem, he worked his mouth and his hand on her sex. Licking and sucking on her clit, hard and swollen. Fucking her with his hand, rubbing that spot inside her that made her—

"More, more, more," she panted, and he laughed before redoubling his efforts. She started to shake around him and he slid in a third finger, stretching her. Filling her until she moaned and grabbed at his head, grinding herself against his face. His cock was painfully hard against the bedspread and he rose up on his knees just enough to reach lower and fist himself with his free hand. Slowly, because he wasn't going to come until he was buried deep inside his woman.

When she exploded, stiffening around him with a series of gorgeous, shaky sounds, he surged up to capture her mouth at the same time as he nudged his cock into her soaking wet pussy, easing himself home.

"I love you," he whispered as she moaned beneath him.

"Love you, too," she panted as she shifted her hips, seating him even deeper in her sex. "Love you so much."

"Well sure, I make you come like a porn star." He groaned as she tightened her pelvic muscles around his dick. "Oh god yeah."

"Two can play that game, high roller." She licked her red, sex-swollen mouth and arched her tits into his chest. "I thought you were going to paddle my ass."

He growled and thrust into her, jerking them both up the bed an inch. "All in good time, vixen."

Her breath hitched and she bit her lip. "Remind me again why I'm going to be punished? Why you're going to turn me over your lap—" Her words were driving him crazy, as intended, and he shifted enough to lift one of her thighs up and press her open, making her gasp for air and then let out a desperate, happy laugh. "Spank me until my ass turns red and pussy starts dripping—"

That did it. He cut her off with a hard, demanding kiss, fucking her in tandem with his tongue and his cock, setting a wicked pace that didn't end until his balls drew tight and his orgasm thudded out of his body, leaving him wasted and heavy on top of Laney.

She laughed, a gentle, loving ripple beneath him.

"What?" he muttered into her neck.

"We still act like this is new. I like it."

He kissed the spot beneath her ear that was guaranteed to make her sigh, then rolled away, kissing her breasts and then her far shoulder as he moved. "I'll never get enough of you. You're like a drug."

"So tell me more about this Graceland Chapel." Laney rolled lazily into Kyle's side. They were both slicked with sweat, but the air-conditioning hummed pleasantly and it wasn't unpleasant. Just productively sticky in a *holy crap look what we just did* kind of way.

"Hmmm?" His voice was thick and full of sleep, but that wouldn't last long. Any second now his stomach would growl and they'd order up some dinner.

"Elvis? You, me, vows…"

He lifted his head and gave her a content smile. "I was just teasing, sweetheart. I thought you were on the other side of the country."

Oh boy, was he in for a surprise. "So you wouldn't want to do that?"

He shrugged and dropped his head to the pillow again. "Sure. Vegas, a beach somewhere…hell, I'd marry you at Chicago City Hall."

"Then let's do it."

It took him a minute to hear the seriousness in her voice, and by the time it hit him she thought her face might split in half from the giant grin she was sporting. "Yeah?"

"Yeah."

"Yeah?" He half-yelled it this time, sleepiness forgotten, and pulled her hard against him. Naked, sweaty, and giddy with excitement, she peppered his face with kisses as he gaped at her. "What about your mom?"

"We'll let them plan a reception for Christmas. But now that my sister's getting married again, I think it's less of a big deal."

He shook his head. "I don't think moms work that way."

She didn't care. "This is just for us. For you. I've been

thinking of you as my husband forever now. Time we make that official."

He slanted his mouth over hers and swept his tongue over her lips, and then inside, hungry and hot all over again. "Damn straight I'm going to make you my wife tonight."

"I'm already your wife," she whispered and he kissed her again.

3
———

"What do you mean we can't get married tonight?"

After eating an extravagant room service dinner, they'd gotten dressed together, bumping elbows in the bathroom and giggling about what they were going to do. Kyle had looked up the marriage bureau address and confirmed they could do a same day service. It looked pretty straightforward.

But now they were at the Graceland Chapel, license in hand, and it was packed. The clerk gave them an apologetic smile. "I'm sorry. We do recommend making a reservation in advance."

Kyle turned to Laney, who looked crushed, and brushed a kiss across her temple. "You want to go somewhere else?" he murmured.

She shrugged. "I'd kind of gotten attached to the idea of being married by Elvis."

The clerk cleared her throat. "We could fit you in at three tomorrow afternoon."

Laney brightened up. "We'll take it."

Disappointment warred with anticipation in his gut. What was one more day? It felt like a lifetime, which was ridiculous.

"Come on, high roller, let's go see if we can find a midnight burlesque show." His almost-wife gave him a naughty smile and his maudlin reaction to the delay was forgotten. Hell yes. He pulled out his phone and texted Willem that he wouldn't be attending the next day's poster display or plenary luncheon. Turned out he had the date of a lifetime instead.

A quick cab ride delivered them to the doors of the hot new dinner theatre where Willem had bought tickets earlier, but it seemed like denial was the order of the day.

"Sorry, man," the ticket seller shrugged. "The midnight show's our most popular. We recommend—"

"Reservations, yeah. I'm getting that vibe loud and clear from this town. Vegas isn't quite what I expected in that regard."

"We do have another show on our smaller stage. A comedy thing. It's weird. And free."

"Wow, you're really selling it."

"The drinks are only two bucks."

Laney groped his ass and whispered something about stripping for him when they got back to the hotel if he bought her a few drinks, but not quietly enough because the ticket guy grinned and told him that sounded like a bang-up deal. Kyle glowered but couldn't deny the truth.

She'd put her black mini-dress back on. Her suitcase had been brought up from the front desk, where she'd left it, and she'd teased him with a glimpse of a leather corset, but she decided she wanted to be able to show their mothers a wedding photo so it had been stashed away again. She'd look good shimmying out of that dress in a bit, and weird and free would at least make for a good story.

And it did. They laughed, and drank, and stumbled out two hours later feeling pretty damn good.

Even though it was the middle of the night back east, Laney texted her sister a picture of them in front of the show poster—both of them flushed and happy. Evie was apparently awake, because she called Laney just as they arrived back at the Venetian. From the half of the conversation he was privy to, he gleaned that their infant niece Ava was teething and waking everyone up at all hours. So Evie was happy to hear about a bit of adult fun in Vegas, but before Laney could wiggle out of the conversation, her too-clever older sister had cottoned on to their secret plan.

"Maybe," Laney said into the phone, biting her lip. Kyle wrapped his arms around her waist and eased her to sit on a stone bench overlooking the man-made canal outside the hotel. "It's just time, you know? And planning a wedding in Wardham when we don't live there—"

She nodded along, still worrying her lip as her sister talked. Kyle braced himself for Evie to talk Laney out of the plan, so when she murmured a few last words and hung up the phone, he didn't say anything. She didn't either, for a minute, just leaned against him.

"There's something about a hot summer night," she said suddenly. Her gaze was fixed straight ahead and he couldn't get a read on what she was thinking from her profile. God, she was gorgeous. Her normally porcelain skin glowed in the lamps overhead, and her shiny hair floated around her head in a loose up-do. Like she'd been spun from gold.

He'd been in love with her all his life and woke up every day thinking it wasn't possible to love her more. And then she'd tell him how she'd helped rebuild someone's face, totally off-the-cuff, like that was something people could just *do*, and he'd fall a little deeper. Or he'd find her cuddling with Buddy on the couch, whispering secret thoughts to their furry companion. And now here they were, about to do something just for them, and he couldn't resent her for having second thoughts, because she just wanted to make their families happy. Deeper. Just like that.

"You want to go for a walk?" he asked, not sure what he wanted the answer to be. Yes, to soak up more of this city that didn't sleep. No, because the privacy of their room beckoned, where they could celebrate their love even if they weren't going to act on the license in his pocket.

As if she hadn't heard his question, she pushed off the bench and headed to the railing. There weren't any gondola rides to be had at this hour, and while people were out and about, quiet sounds filled the warm air around them. The water below Laney lapped gently against the walls of the canal. In the distance, cars sped up and slowed down. And ten feet away from him, Kyle's almost-wife sighed.

"What I want," she said, turning back to face him, her hands outstretched, "is to marry you tomorrow at three in the afternoon. Invited guests will include Elvis and any hobos we stumble across on the way there."

He leaped up and took her hands, twirling her into a close embrace, her back nestled against his front. "And our families?"

"They'll get to see the pictures." She hummed a few bars from an old Alan Jackson song, one of her favourites, and he rocked her in his arms.

"Want to dance?" She nodded and he spun her into position. They did this pretty often—usually in their kitchen, not in the courtyard of a hotel, but spontaneous dancing was spontaneous dancing. Sort of their thing. And a total turn-on for Laney. Ergo, a no-brainer for Kyle.

The hem of her dress slid up and down his thigh as they turned and twisted together. The temptation to drop his hand and play with the bare skin of her leg proved irresistible. Instead of batting his hand away, she hooked her leg around his, freezing them in a locked together stance. She stroked her fingertips up and down his neck for a moment, just staring into his eyes, and what could have been totally cheesy was actually totally perfect.

———

"YOU WANT to take me back to your room for that striptease, high roller?" Laney desperately wanted to lighten the mood. She didn't know how Kyle dealt with all the big feelings he had.

"Is that your way of dodging around whatever heavy thoughts are in your head?"

"Wow, got it in one. Impressive." She licked along his jaw. "Can I distract you by promising Canadian rules for the stripping?"

He laughed. "Sweetheart, you naked is awesome, but it's not new and shiny anymore. I'm not so easily distracted. Talk to me."

Where to start. A weird ache made itself known in her chest and she sighed. "You know what my sister said? 'Is that the kind of wedding you want to tell your grandkids about?'"

"Ahhh." He kissed her forehead and smiled down at her. God, he undid her with his constant understanding. "Well, it's the kind of wedding I'm happy to tell my mom about, which I think is sort of the same question. Point is, is it the kind of wedding *you* want?"

"Just you and me?" This was steadier ground. "Absolutely. Because that's what it might be for us—there might not be kids and grandkids. But…" She hadn't trailed off because the words were hard to find. She just didn't know if she was being silly or not. He waited, just being the usual big, strong, rock of her life. "I do want a dress."

He teased one finger under the skinny strap and tugged it down, taking her bra strap with it. He kissed her bare shoulder, sending shivers down her spine. "I like this dress."

"I want a lacy dress and flowers. Maybe blue shoes." He licked along her collarbone to the hollow at the base of her neck, and she sucked in a needy breath. "Can we go shopping in the morning?"

"We can do whatever you want, wife-of-mine." He found her mouth, kissing her with abandon. Around them, the Las Vegas night faded away and she moaned, unable to hold back.

"Let me take you to bed, Laney," he whispered, pressing their foreheads together. "I'll show you just how perfect we are, no matter what."

Back in their room, they quietly stripped and brushed their teeth side-by-side. There was no urgency, just a heady promise that their bed was waiting for them. And when they tumbled into it, hot with the knowledge that the next day was their wedding day, the love they made was sweet and slow and, indeed, quite perfect.

LANEY WOKE FIRST. They hadn't drawn the blackout blinds, so warm sun hit her face around eight and she sat up like a shot. *Holy crap, we're getting married.* She looked at Kyle, flopped out on his stomach, sleeping like a baby. An overgrown, gorgeous baby with a tight butt and slightly unruly golden brown hair, now starting to fleck with silver threads. *When did that happen?* She pressed a gentle kiss between his shoulder blades and reached for the phone to order some breakfast.

She heard the knock as she was getting out of the shower, then the low rumble of Kyle's voice as he tipped the waiter.

"You smell yummy," he said as they kissed good morning.

"Special wedding moisturizer."

"That's a thing?"

She laughed. "It's just something I bought in O'Hare while I was waiting for my flight. I like the idea that this scent will forever be tied to this trip in my memory."

He lifted his brows in surprise. "Laney Calhoun, how sentimental of you!"

"I—" Yeah, she couldn't really claim she was normally like that. "I guess it's your good influence."

He winked and passed her a cup of coffee. "So, shopping?"

"Will you want to buy something too?"

"I should. I didn't pack anything really nice."

The night before he'd worn dark blue jeans and a white dress shirt, with the sleeves rolled up. He'd looked scrumptious, but the thought of him in a suit made her tingle. "It might take a while to find stuff off the rack. We should probably head in different directions. Meet back here?"

"Sure. I need to talk to the front desk about extending this reservation anyway."

"Already done." She snagged a piece of bacon off his plate and munched. "You've got the license…I'll leave the rings here so I'm not carting them all over town."

He reached across the table and looped his fingers through hers. "I love that you brought them with you."

"We should have used them sooner." She offered a small smile.

"Nope. This feels right."

It really did.

An hour later, she was wandering around the Grand Shoppes, sipping a chai latte and waiting for Barney's to open. She had the store's website open on her phone and she was hoping against hope that they'd have the pale blue Manolo Blahnik pumps she'd already fallen in love with. She'd never spent more than two hundred dollars on a pair of shoes, and those had been special clogs to wear in the operating room. But these shoes…she was in love.

She stopped in front of the women's clothing store, Bebe, because a gorgeous tapioca coloured dress in the window caught her eye. A young woman slid the doors open. "Are you looking for something? I can open a little early."

A wide smile slid across Laney's face. "Do you sell white dresses?"

The other woman laughed. "Getting married today? Come on in."

Laney tried on three lace dresses, but her attention kept slipping back to the burnished cream dress in the window.

"Do you want to try that one on as well?" The sales-girl, Chastity, wiggled her eyebrows. "This is Vegas. All rules are tossed out the window."

"Yes. Why the heck not."

As soon as Laney smoothed the bandage dress down over her hips, she knew it was the one. "Do you think this will go with blue shoes?"

Chastity nodded. "I think it would go with flip flops on you, honey. You look gorgeous."

By the time she paid and made it to the shoe depart-ment at Barney's, the department store was hopping. She found a saleslady and explained what she was looking for. Eighteen agonizing minutes later, the woman came out of the back room nervously holding a white shoe box. "We don't have a 38. I'm hoping that because they fit small, this 38.5 will be perfect for you."

Butterflies all abuzz in her tummy, Laney slid off her sandals and nervously slid her foot into the leather pump. Surprisingly, it was almost too snug. She could feel her face falling and tried to bravely hide her disap-pointment. "That's okay, thanks for trying."

"Oh no, that's how it's supposed to fit!" The woman

clapped her hands together. "They'll stretch to your foot."

"But I'm getting married today," Laney whispered. She didn't have time for fancy shoes to get used to *her*. "Is there a bigger size?"

"They'd be too big within a few hours. These will be perfect. What are a few blisters on your wedding day, then? And you'll wear them again and again."

Maybe only in her bedroom. She held her breath and nodded. The dress hadn't been that expensive. This was a once in a lifetime event. And they were ever so pretty. Blisters be damned.

The older woman leaned forward with a conspiratorial wink. "Stop at the Estée Lauder counter. Ask for Jackie. Tell her Maria says this pretty bride deserves a little pampering today."

So that's exactly what Laney did. Jackie tweezed her eyebrows and applied flawless makeup, and only accepted payment for the tube of lipstick Laney took with her back to the room.

Kyle wasn't there, but a quick glance at her phone told her it was just past one and they still had plenty of time. She hung up her dress in front of the window, then gleefully arranged her shoes underneath it and snapped a few pictures. She texted one to Evie. The response was swift. **Are you going to call Mom? I mean, wheeee! And are you going to call Mom?**

She should. She would. They could do that together, maybe, her and Kyle.

She dug through her suitcase. Lingerie was the one thing she hadn't needed to buy today, because she'd had the set she wanted to wear for months now. *Even if I dragged my feet, it wasn't because I didn't want this with every fibre of my being.* Pale blue lace underwear, the same shade as the shoes, and a strapless bra, satin, with touch of the same lace between the cups.

The shoes taunted her from across the room. Nervously, she stepped into them, hoping that she wasn't going to end up limping through their planned night of dinner and dancing. Just then, the door opened and she whirled around.

Kyle loomed in the doorway, and her entire being turned to liquid desire. "Oh, wow," she breathed. He was wearing a black suit, fitted, with a white dress shirt and a skinny black tie. He'd gotten a haircut and a shave, and he looked *slick*. "You…look…oh, baby."

He slowed to a stop and gave her a hungry once over. From the heavy eyelids and how he was biting his lower lip, she knew he liked what little she was wearing, too.

"Don't even think of tackling me, mister. This took a lot of work." She put an extra sway in her step as she moved toward the side table for her jewelry, relieved that the shoes worked. "Besides, you're done. I'm still a work in progress."

"I can't imagine you improving on how you look right now, Lane." He winked, then looked down at his suit. "So…you like?"

"I *like* how you look in a plaid shirt and jeans. This is something special."

He blushed and that made him even hotter. "I called Liam. He talked me into flat front pants."

"Yeah. We should buy you more of those."

He held out his arms and she crossed the room, desperate for his touch but also aware of her careful makeup application. "The face," she warned gently.

He nodded, stroking his hands down her arms and then back up her sides, growling ever so slightly as he cupped her breasts. Even through the satin, her nipples beaded at the ministrations of his thumbs. "I won't touch your face," he promised, dropping to his knees. He kissed his way down her sternum, and she held him against her for a moment before he pressed back up, leaving one last kiss at the apex of her neck and her shoulder. "I can't wait to strip these off of you."

"Me, too." She licked her lips. "Help me cover them up first, though?"

He nodded.

4

———

Kyle had apparently stopped at the concierge desk and arranged for a private town car for the rest of the day. Their driver, Hassan, was waiting for them outside and took them on a bit of a drive around the city on the way to the chapel. Laney had heard women talk about their wedding day passing in a blur but didn't expect that to apply to her. The surreal feeling that they were really doing this took her completely by surprise. She wasn't nervous, exactly. Her pulse was slow and steady, but crazy loud inside her head. Her hands were damp with perspiration and she was having trouble paying attention to the things Kyle pointed out as they whisked through the streets.

"Shouldn't there be more traffic?" she blurted out, and the two men laughed.

"People are at work. I know the streets. You're a bit

distracted." Hassan winked at her in the rear-view mirror.

"I am that," she murmured.

Kyle picked up her hand and drew light circles on each of her knuckles. "I'm nervous as well."

"It's not nerves, exactly."

He laughed. "Good, because I was totally lying."

His laughter…yes, she needed more of that. "Tell me this is what you want. Me, forever."

He brought her hand to his mouth and kissed her fingers with sweet reverence. "Forever. You and me. Buddy, and maybe another fur ball to keep him company. Kids are entirely optional. I promise you are everything I want."

She spun her hand around and cupped his jaw. "I adore you so much, Kyle Nixon. I have since high school, and I still can't believe that we found our way back to each other."

"Believe it, Laney. This is really happening."

From the front seat, Hassan cleared his throat. "If you don't mind me interjecting, it's five to three. It's really happening…right now."

Feeling more centred and ready for anything, Laney smoothed her skirt as Kyle jogged around the car to help her out.

Inside the chapel, the clerk gave her a small bouquet of red roses and a boutonniere which she pinned to Kyle's lapel. Hassan happily took her phone and snapped a few photos before promising to record the entire service.

"We forgot the hobos," Kyle whispered as they walked to the front of the room. Laney had resolutely refused to have Elvis walk her down the aisle.

"Boo, and here I thought it was perfect." Another thought occurred to her, this one tinged with regret that it didn't come up sooner, and she paused midway up the aisle.

"What?" Kyle turned and looked at her with concern.

"We should call our mothers. And put this on speaker phone."

"Are you sure?"

She nodded. "If you don't mind…"

"I don't mind." He closed the gap between them and kissed her gently. "Whatever you want."

"No." She shook her head. "Whatever *you* want. Do you want this to just be the two of us?"

"And Hassan and Elvis, but not our mothers? I'd never live that down."

She turned to get her phone back from Hassan, and he already had his out. "I'll record on mine and email you the file."

She squeezed his hand. "Thank you."

In front of them, Elvis cleared his throat. "We just about ready here, folks? Love waits for no man, ya hear me?"

Kyle held up his hand, completely undeterred by the six and a half foot tall impersonator. "One more thing."

They dialed at the same time. Kyle laced his fingers into hers.

Claire answered first. "Laney, I'm just about head into town, can this wait?"

She laughed. "Not really. Kyle and I have some exciting news. We've eloped. Well, we're eloping. Currently. And I thought you might want to listen to the service."

In the dead silence that followed, she heard Kyle having a very similar conversation with his mother, but her reaction was louder and made him laugh.

"Mom?"

"Delaney Calhoun, this is wonderful news."

"Oh my god. Mom, are you crying?"

"Well of course I'm crying, you ninny! I thought you were going to be shacked up with Kyle forever!"

"Okay, well, that's…good. Good. Okay. I'm going to put you on speaker phone now, and Elvis is going to—"

"Elvis? Goodness. Well—"

Laney hit speaker phone even as her mother continued to react and set the phone down on the front pew. Kyle did the same, then took her hands.

Elvis, who had apparently seen it all, shrugged and starting singing.

The service was short. A song, some jokes, and before she knew it, Elvis was tapping Kyle on the shoulder. "You going alone on this one, my man?"

———

No way in hell was he using Elvis's words to marry Laney. "I've got this."

She was shaking like a leaf, and he wanted to pull her close. *Fuck it*, this was his wedding. He did just that. "Sweetheart, this has been such a long time coming. But the waiting makes it even sweeter, I promise. And this is how we do things. Spontaneous. Surprising. A little weird. And together."

She slid her hands up his chest and around his neck. "I love you," she whispered.

"I promise I'll never get tired of hearing that."

"I promise to say it every day."

"I promise to make you coffee," he said quietly, loving how she got all that meant—that he supported her early mornings and late nights, her overnight shifts and every cancelled plan.

"I promise to wash your gym clothes without complaining."

"I promise to iron your dress shirts."

She smiled and whispered, "I promise to wear *your* dress shirts."

"I promise to always think you're beautiful in them."

She'd stopped shaking. She paused before her next vow, and when she spoke again, her voice was strong and clear. "I'll support you in everything you do."

Damn, now it was his turn to be overtaken by emotion. He cleared his throat. "I'll be by your side in good times and bad."

Her eyes warmed at that one. He didn't want there to

be any bad times, but if there were, they'd handle them together.

"Delaney Calhoun, I promise you forever."

"And I promise you forever, too, Kyle Nixon." She lifted on her tiptoes and kissed him soundly.

Elvis hummed a bar of music, then chuckled. "That's got me all shook up, I gotta say. What do you say we make it all official in the State of Nevada? I now pronounce you husband and wife. Go on, give the little lady another kiss."

Laney rolled her eyes and laughed, but she stopped laughing as soon as he dipped her back and gave her a kiss that made Elvis blush. Kyle assumed Elvis was blushing, anyway. He couldn't see anyone but his bride.

WHAT ONCE WAS HOME

FOREWORD

The best laid plans...

What Once Was Home is a second short story sequel to *What Once Was Perfect*. It takes place after *When They Weren't Looking*, Laney's sister's book, and contains significant spoilers. Go and read that book first if you haven't yet!

1

———

mid January

Laney rolled her eyes and forced herself not to smile as she pulled clothes from her dresser and tossed them toward her suitcase, open on the bed.

Kyle cleared his throat. "Laney…"

"Kyle…" This time she couldn't keep the grin at bay. She turned around and sighed, leaning back against the solid wood dresser. It was sweet that he worried. She smoothed her hands over her slight belly bump and looked him straight in the eye, no more kidding around. "I'll drive safely."

She was heading to their hometown, Wardham, five hours away, for a baby shower, and was going to fit in some work while she was in the area. There was a promising plastic surgery resident doing a rotation an hour away from Wardham, in a community hospital, that

Laney's colleagues wanted to recruit to their practice at the children's hospital here in Chicago.

Kyle didn't care that it made the most sense to leave now, while she was fresh. Even after two years, he didn't get how turned upside down her internal clock could get. He gave her a puppy dog look that almost worked. "Go in the morning."

"I slept all day. This is my morning."

"And it's dark and dangerous out there." His gaze dropped to her belly. "Humour me."

"It'll be hard for me to go back to sleep for a while." She'd come off a twenty-four hour shift at seven that morning. Hadn't gotten home until after nine, and by the time she fed herself and showered, she hadn't hit the hay until ten. And the baby kept her asleep until dinnertime. "It makes the most sense—"

She didn't get a chance to finish her sentence, because Kyle had pushed himself off the bed in one fluid motion and was crowding her against the dresser. She ran her hands over the warm flannel of his untucked shirt and tipped her head back, letting him rain gentle kisses along her neck. The fuzz of his three-day-old beard scratched all her nerve endings to life in that give-him-whatever-he-wants kind of way.

"You know I'm not rational about you and our little bean, right?" He nipped at her ear, his fingers threading through her hair as he held her in place. "I should come with you."

"But you've got two papers due and you have to teach on Monday. If you came with me, then I wouldn't be able to go to Bluewater Cove to meet this resident. We've been over this." She arched her back as he trailed one hand down her side, his palm grazing her hypersensitive breast on the way. It wouldn't be long before he had her shirt off and her bra tugged low. Her boobs had never been this big in her entire life. They were both enjoying that, although it was fine line between pleasure and pain.

"I don't care. I'll call in sick," he growled, sliding the elastic waist of her maternity pants lower on her hips. She rolled her eyes back in her head as he squeezed her hip. His hands were warm and strong. Each possessive touch undid her, until she was a million pieces of want and her resolve had fled their little bungalow. No, he couldn't come with her, but she could give him the night drive.

"Fine, I'll go in the morning," she whispered. "But you need to tire me out and put me back to bed."

She could feel his grin, wicked and full of himself, against her neck. "Deal."

———

THE NEXT MORNING, Kyle made his wife a travel mug of coffee and gave her a long, lingering kiss goodbye before following her out to her car, Buddy in tow on his leash. They watched her drive off into the early dawn. It was damn early, but that was the price he'd pay for keeping Laney home last night.

Worth every extra cup of coffee he'd chug. But first, the dog park. Buddy needed a good workout this morning, because Kyle had a long day of work ahead of him.

Back inside an hour later, he looked longingly at his PlayStation. That would have to wait. He'd negotiated with himself—an hour of the latest Batman game when he finished his first paper. Two hours and a beer when he finished the second. A pizza and as much game-time as the weekend allowed once he was done both and his lesson plan for Monday was sorted out.

And still he worried about Laney, and wanted to be with her in the car for the long drive home.

Chicago had given him more than he ever expected—love, first and foremost. So much love, he couldn't believe it. And now they were having a baby. He looked around their three bedroom house. They never used their spare bedroom, so that would get turned into the nursery. Laney's office would remain untouched. They had a nice fenced backyard, perfect for toddlers and dogs alike.

This house, and their life here, was perfect in almost every way.

The fact that they were six hours from every member of their family was still hard for him. He kept that buried deep down inside, because it paled in comparison to how important his wife was. Laney was his everything, and wherever she went, he would follow without a second thought.

Without regret.

Five months, he muttered under his breath.

He'd finish his Masters degree in Education in the summer. Then he'd be free to make all the drives back and forth with her. He squared his shoulders and headed for the coffee pot. Maybe if he lost himself in his paper on post-humanist theory, the time would pass and before he'd know it, she'd be sending him a text that she'd arrived.

———

"HOLY SHIT, YOU'VE POPPED!"

Laney rolled her eyes at her older sister. "Why are you surprised? You've done this three times. It's what usually happens, no?"

"I know, but we *just* saw you at Christmas, and you weren't like…that." Evie pointed at Laney's belly.

It was true. Somewhere around New Year's, she'd lost the ability to pass as just being addicted to cheese. Although that was true, too. Baby liked Gouda. Now she had a solid basketball under her snug, long-sleeved t-shirt. "I was also wearing dressier blouses over the holidays. In hindsight, an excellent move. What is it about a woman being pregnant that turns everyone into Handsy McHandsys?"

Evie made a shushing should as she reached for the belly.

"See?"

Her sister just laughed and gave her future niece or nephew a rub. "Hey Little Bean." Evie glanced up. "You're really not going to find out if it's a boy or a girl?"

"Nope." They could find out, of course. Laney had done all the prenatal screening available, including CVS, which would definitively provide gender.

If they wanted to know.

Which they didn't.

So it sat there in the report at her OB's office, a little secret.

From her purse, her phone dinged. "Can you grab that for me? It'll be Kyle."

Evie passed it over, then headed for their mother's kitchen. "You want tea?"

"Sounds great." Laney answered automatically. She read Kyle's response—**Glad you made it. I hate school**—and laughed. Then she realized it was her hippie-dippie sister making the tea, and thought she should clarify just exactly what was on offer. She lifted her voice. "Wait, is it made of grass?"

No response. She tossed her overnight bag onto the steps, and followed her sister into the kitchen.

"Evie?"

Her sister stuck out her tongue. "Red raspberry leaf tea. Excellent uterine tonic."

"That doesn't sound like it's been tested in a double blind study. Keep your woo-woo tea away from me."

"It's nice with honey."

"Is that code for, 'tastes like grass without honey'?"

Evie laughed and pulled the boxed of orange pekoe tea down from the cupboard. "I'll make you regular tea, maybe."

"Good plan." Laney hugged her sister from behind, the Bean pressing into her sister's back. "Why does Mom have raspberry leaf tea, anyway?"

"Leftover from when I had Ava?"

Evie turning that into a question totally gave her away and Laney squeezed more gently this time. "How far along are you?"

"Just found out two weeks ago." Evie twisted her head, pressing their cheeks together, and the sisters shared a quiet moment of glee. "Hopefully it sticks and our babies will be the same age."

"Wow." Laney grinned. "Congratulations."

"Thank you. But we're keeping it quiet. Mom might have guessed, because I've had two naps here in the last week, but she hasn't said anything."

"Mum's the word."

Evie twisted around and squeezed her sister's hand. "Mom times two."

"Oh, psssht. Kyle will be more the mom than I will." As soon as she said it, she wanted to claw the words back. It wasn't true. She already loved her Little Bean with all her heart. That surprised her more than anything. She'd never wanted this, not hungrily like her sister had. Not until she'd felt that tiny, growing thing inside her, and now it was her reason for being.

Evie saw right through her. Her sister winked and

just handed over the tea. They talked about names and surviving fatigue, and when their mother came in, moved the conversation effortlessly to the farm and Claire's plan to rent out the fields again for the growing season.

But after Evie's husband, Liam, arrived with their three children, and they'd had a boisterous dinner, when Laney was alone in her childhood bedroom and texting now and then with Kyle, but mostly leaving him alone because he still hadn't figured out the last bit of his first paper and he needed the quiet…that was when Laney's thoughts turned back to the conversation with her sister.

Their babies might be the same age. But how close would they be, growing up in two different countries, a six-hour drive apart?

2

____

Eloping had meant that Laney didn't have to have a bridal shower, but with two eager grandmothers and two overachieving aunts, the baby shower couldn't be avoided.

And she was a lucky woman for it. Now that the whirlwind Sunday afternoon party was winding to a close, she was extraordinarily glad she'd acquiesced to her family's request to spoil her just a little. She'd never felt quite so loved and fawned over. The baby had more sleepers and diapers and knit hats than he or she would ever need—although maybe just enough, if some of the spitting up stories were true. And Laney had been spoiled as well. Chocolate for now, wine for later, and promises from all to come to Chicago and help.

In an orderly, scheduled fashion, even.

That had brought tears to her eyes, although it seemed like it didn't take much these days.

Now as the party wound down, she leaned back on her sister-in-law's couch and took everything in. There was yellow and white tissue paper everywhere and the dessert table was mostly picked over. Laney herself had eaten enough lemon squares to push herself into that uncomfortably full feeling. Baby seemed to like the blast of sugar, though, and she realized she had an opportunity to be an exceptionally good daughter-in-law. She caught Kyle's mother's eye.

"Baby's kicking, Eleanor." She pointed to her belly. "If you want to feel it?"

They weren't overly close, mostly because of geographical distance, but she liked her mother-in-law. The warmth in her chest increased as Eleanor settled in next to her and, instead of reaching straight for the belly, looked Laney in the eye instead. "How are you doing?"

She smiled, hoping it reached her eyes. "I'm good."

"Is my son being insufferably overprotective?"

Laney laughed, the smile more real this time as she thought of her husband, hard at work and worrying about her at the same time. "A little. I like it, though. He loves this little person so much already. That's amazing, right?"

"It is." Eleanor dropped her hand, hovering her fingers above Laney's shirt. "May I?"

Laney nodded and pointed at the most pronounced bump. "That's either a head or bum, I'm not sure. It'll roll in a minute. It's pretty cool."

"I imagine the drives back and forth will get harder

soon," her mother-in-law said quietly. "We'll have to come to see you."

But the baby was due at the end of April. Right in the middle of corn planting. Laney tried to swallow and couldn't. Hot tears sprang into her eyes, and Eleanor made a gentle shushing sound.

"It's fine."

"Planting season…"

"Will carry on without me. I haven't driven a tractor since the boys were teenagers. And they can make their own mid-day meal."

Laney sniffled as she laughed. "Oh, the horror."

"Right?" Eleanor gasped as the baby moved under her hand, then rubbed gently, more for mommy than baby, Laney figured. "It'll be just fine. I remember being so scared when I was pregnant with Ian. I kept having a recurring dream that I'd left him at the store, and I couldn't remember his name. What new mother doesn't know her own baby's name?"

"I have a dream like that, too," Laney whispered. She couldn't even tell Kyle about it, but something about her mother-in-law's confession gave her the courage to share as well. "I take Bean to surgery with me and leave him or her in my locker."

Eleanor laughed. "It's every woman's fear. That we're going to be terrible mothers. But you know what? You're going to be just fine. I was. Your mother was. Carrie and Evie are, right?"

"Yes." But Laney didn't feel like everyone else. She

hadn't wanted this like they had. She did *now*, of course. She closed her eyes. *I want you so much, Little Bean,* she promised silently. But what if she'd put off having kids because she didn't have that maternal urge? What if that was a sign?

———

"ARE you sleeping at your mom's again tonight?"

Laney smiled as Kyle's warm voice worked its way into her heart. "Yeah. I went over to the schoolhouse to do some quiet work this morning, but I didn't want to buy any groceries. And it's kind of rude to eat here but sleep there."

The real reason was that one of their mothers had been into the renovated house and washed the sheets, so they didn't smell like her husband. If that faint memory of Kyle had still been imprinted from their visit over the holiday, she'd have stayed there. Or brought a pillow over to her mom's, although it would have been a toss-up. She loved the little turn-of-the-last-century school-house that he'd bought and slowly turned into a home before they got back together, and was so glad they'd decided to keep it as a second home when he'd moved to Chicago.

But it wasn't quite the same without him.

Nothing was. She closed her eyes and urged him to keep talking. "Tell me about your lesson for tomorrow."

"I'll send you the slide deck."

She laughed at how he totally missed the point. "Okay. But still tell me about it. I like listening to your voice."

"I like listening to yours, too. Tell me more about those lemon squares."

"Oh my God, don't get me started. I brought three back with me, I might need to go raid the kitchen. Carrie is freaking artist with sugar."

"Tease."

"If you keep talking to me until I fall asleep, then I might save one for you."

"No way will it last until Tuesday. You and the Bean don't have that kind of will power. Nobody does."

She laughed. "Okay, I'll pull the pregnant lady card and ask Carrie to make another tray."

"A double tray."

"Deal." She smiled and closed her eyes again as he lowered his voice and told her about his lesson plan for the next day. At some point in the middle of an explanation about the small group discussion he hoped to get going, she drifted off into a blissfully dreamless sleep.

IF YOU COUNTED BEING a swim instructor and lifeguard in high school, Kyle had been teaching for nearly twenty years, fourteen of those as an elementary school teacher. And he was still nervous about his guest lecture to the B.Ed. class. He wasn't just talking to them, teacher to teacher, about the realities and challenges of managing a classroom—that he could do in his sleep. Today he was giving them a lecture that he could get behind, in theory, but in reality was fraught with problems. But he was being graded on this lesson by an old-school prof who wouldn't take kindly to the "get real" version of the lecture that was racing around in Kyle's head.

The one he'd accidentally told Laney about the night before, although she may have fallen asleep before he got to the meat of it.

He'd arrived in the classroom twenty minutes early, so his laptop was already hooked up and his name was written on the whiteboard.

Kyle Nixon, M Ed class of 2016
Guest Lecturer

He watched the students file in. Some of them looked tired. Others distracted, either by conversation or technology.

None of them looked interested in the least, and he couldn't blame them. They were halfway through their intensive program and they all just wanted to be out doing practicums, learning from teachers on the job.

He remembered these bullshit lessons from his own undergrad degree. Had sort of forgotten them in the last year and a half, as he'd sunk into the conversations with peers that really cared and instructors who pushed them to the next level.

But right now, it all came racing back, and he knew they weren't going to like his lecture. Hell, he wasn't going to like his lecture.

The clock ticked to the top of the hour, and his pulse slammed in his throat.

He took a step forward and cleared his throat. "Good morning, everyone." He pointed at the white board. "I'm Kyle Nixon…"

And then he knew what he needed to do. He stepped back and grabbed a red marker. He added the most important piece of information to the board in big block letters.

Kyle Nixon, M Ed class of 2016
Guest Lecturer
GRADE 4/5/6 TEACHER
(14 LONG, WONDERFUL YEARS)

"And I'm a teacher. I'm taking a break from the class-room to do some graduate work, but my pedagogy begins and ends in the classroom, where it matters. And that's what we're going to talk about for the next hour." He took a deep breath, refusing to look to the back of the lecture hall where his professor sat. "So let's talk about all the ways that what we're taught in here has zero bearing on what we see out there."

He might be fucking over his career as an academic, but at least he had everyone's attention.

3

———

Laney had never been to Bluewater Cove Regional Medical Centre before, and she was surprised when, after driving for an hour on county roads surrounded by snow-covered fields and not much else, she found herself in the parking lot of a substantial hospital.

Even though a surgical resident was doing a rotation here, she'd thought it would be smaller than *this*. A large central tower, the hospital also had two significant-sized wings, and it was all gleaming bright and shiny in the winter sun. She parked in the visitor lot and headed inside. A friendly volunteer at a desk in the lobby pointed the way to the OR, where she introduced herself to the coordinator in the front office. He looked at the schedule and informed her that the resident, Dr. Kim, would be in surgery for another thirty minutes.

Before she finished writing a note for Dr. Kim, she heard a voice behind her. "Laney Calhoun?"

She looked up and saw a tall, familiar form from her past. "Wyatt!" She gave her former classmate a big grin and took his extended hand. "I didn't know you were here!"

Wyatt Fisher had been a year ahead of her in medical school, and had done one rotation at the hospital she did her residency at in Calgary. "Long time no see."

"Did you know I'd be here?"

He winked. The man was walking charisma, although it had never been like that between them. And it wasn't now, either. His gaze was curious and looked on her, but not in an *interested* way. "Ellie told me she was interviewing with you and I thought I'd surprise you. Can I buy you a coffee?"

She tipped her head to the side, trying to read him. It was impossible. But coffee sounded great. "Of course."

They fell into step beside each other as he directed her to the coffee shop on the third floor. The lounge looked out the other side of the hospital from where she'd parked, and she gasped at the view—in front of them lay the town of Bluewater Cove, and beyond that, the frozen edge of Lake Huron.

"Nice, huh?"

Laney looked out the window again after they got drinks and a bagel for baby. "This is some hospital you've got here, Dr. Fisher. I'm assuming you're on staff?"

"Not just on staff. As of two weeks ago, I'm the interim chief of surgery."

"Wow." It wasn't uncommon for young surgeons to get pushed into leadership roles. They were often thankless positions that older surgeons had done their time in and wanted nothing more to do with. "That's a lot of work."

"Especially when we're short-staffed."

She couldn't imagine. "Cancelling surgeries?"

"Some. Doing a lot in the evenings and on weekends, too. Just a lot of hours." He rocked back in his chair. His gaze never left her face. "How are you liking Chicago?"

She hesitated.

He shrugged. "You can tell me to piss off if you want."

She laughed. "No, I like it a lot. *We* like it. My husband is actually from around here…"

From the twinkle in Wyatt's eye, he knew that.

Laney gave him an "I see what you're doing" look, and kept going. "But he's moved to Chicago and is in the middle of grad school there. We really do like it, but…the answer is more complicated now than it used to be." She pointed at her belly. "I'm due in the spring."

Wyatt nodded slowly. "And what's your plan for returning to work after the baby is born?"

She rubbed the spot between her eyebrows that always pinched tight when she thought about this. "I'll be back to work pretty soon. That's our life, right? But we'll balance it as best we can."

"Ever think about moving back to Canada?"

She took a deep breath. "And where would I find a hospital that wanted to hire a paediatric plastic surgeon?"

His grin returned, bigger than before, and spread his arms out wide. "Maybe right here."

———

"And then he said…"

Kyle rolled his eyes as his friend Willem recounted how Kyle's lecture went to two of their colleagues. The bastard hadn't even been in his class. "That's not exactly—"

Willem kept going, and Kyle kicked back, rocking on his chair's back legs. It was entertaining, anyway.

He often missed out on these extended discussions that spilled into department pub nights, because his first choice would always be to head home to his wife.

But since Laney was gone, Kyle was free to stay and be roasted, apparently. He waved the waitress over and ordered another pitcher of beer.

Not that Laney would ever begrudge him being social.

Not at all.

Kyle's desire to be at home with her was all on him, and his primitive caveman instincts which had reared up *hard* since Laney found out she was pregnant.

He grinned to himself.

A baby. Shit, he still couldn't quite believe it.

"What are you so happy about, man? You said Professor Richards got up and left before you were even done."

Kyle shrugged. At the end of the day, did it really matter if got reprimanded? "What is he going to do, block me from continuing in the program? I'd grieve that so hard to the Dean." He blew a raspberry. "Maybe I won't get a letter of recommendation to do my doctoral program, but I'm taking a year off to raise my kid next year. It doesn't matter."

And maybe when he decided to go back to work, he might want to be back in the classroom.

Might.

Ha. More like definitely wanted that.

He needed to have a heart-to-heart with Laney when she got home. Figure out the best option for getting him licensed to teach in Illinois. Right now he was in the States on a student visa, and when that came to an end, he'd be eligible to stay as Laney's spouse. But getting a regular work visa would be more complicated. And also not what he really needed to be worried about right now, but with the baby on the way, all of his "take charge" instincts were on high-alert.

His phone vibrated in his pocket. Speak of the beautiful devil. He pulled it out and angled away from his friends. "Hello, my wife."

Laney made a happy sighing sound in his ear. "Hello, my husband."

"You back at your mom's farm?"

"Yep." She yawned in his ear. "Ended up spending the entire day in Bluewater Cove and going out with some of the surgeons."

"That sounds promising. How'd your meeting go? Do you like the resident?"

"Ellie Kim? Yeah, she's great. I'll recommend she come to Chicago for a short rotation, see how she fits with the team."

"That's awesome."

"Mmm-hmmm. But it's not why I called. Oh! Wait, how did your lecture go?"

He'd texted her a non-update update at lunchtime, but he hadn't wanted to distract her with the fact that he'd been a bit reckless. "Yeah…you know. It went."

"What does that mean?"

"Nothing. What was the other thing you wanted to talk about?"

She laughed. "How not-so-deftly you change the subject."

"Brute force, baby."

"Ah. You don't want to talk about it?"

"I'm at the pub with the guys."

"Oh. Okay. Sorry. I'll…we can talk later." But there was something in her voice that said the other thing was worth talking about *now*.

"Sweetie, it's fine." He shoved away from the table and wandered to the front window of the pub, away from the noise of his friends talking shop. "My lecture went a bit off the rails. It was good, actually, in that everyone was engaged. But bad, in a way, because I said some stuff. About academia being bullshit."

"Oh my God. For real?" She gasped, then sighed. "Well, it's kind of true."

"Right?"

"Of course, right. I've got your back. I'm sure you said what needed to be said."

Her words meant more than anything else. He rubbed his chest. Even after all they'd been through, sometimes he was surprised by the ferocity of her love for him. She was going to be an awesome mom, and she really had no clue that he could see that so clearly. "Okay, I shared. Your turn."

"Well..." She sighed, sleepiness roll off the single word and turning to a cloud of nothing. He pictured her rolling onto her back and closing her eyes. She lowered her voice and mumbled something.

"What? I didn't catch that."

She cleared her throat. "My mom is moving around outside and I'm trying to be quiet. And I'm zonked, even though I didn't do much today."

"It's something you don't want your mom to know about?"

"Not yet." He heard rustling. "I'm hiding under my blanket now. So mature. Kyle, they've offered me a job. In Bluewater Cove. We can move home."

4

———————

At first Laney thought the phone connection had broken, because Kyle didn't say anything. She tried again. "They're offering me a permanent staff position, too. Not a locum."

"A job." His voice was flat, and she desperately wish she'd FaceTimed him instead of calling. The pub noise in the background didn't help, either. "Are you serious?"

"Of course."

"When do you need to give them a decision?"

"We can take our time. Probably a few weeks."

The silence on the other end of the line wasn't what she'd expected, and she tried to figure out what the problem was. She gentled her voice. "We won't move until you're done school."

He huffed roughly in her ear. "That's so far from my thoughts right now, sweetheart."

"Then why aren't you…I mean, aren't you excited?"

"This isn't a good time to be making drastic decisions, Laney."

"It's not a drastic decision."

"We'd be moving *countries*."

She rolled her eyes. That was overstating the situation a bit. "Sure, technically. But we'd be moving *home*."

"This is our home now. You're not thinking clearly."

"I'm not—" She pulled the phone away from her head and glared at it. *What?* She cleared her throat and counted backwards from ten. She got to seven before she snapped. "What the hell does that mean?"

"Uhhh…." His swallow was pretty damn loud. All of Chicago probably heard it. "I've said the wrong thing."

"I just got offered the job we've both been waiting for, and you want me to turn it down because I'm *not thinking clearly?*" Okay, when her voice tipped up into a shriek like that, maybe he had a point. But *still*. "This is a dream opportunity, Kyle."

"Is it?" He ignored her next yip of protest and kept going. "Okay, first of all, I didn't say that you should turn it down. And I'm not denying that I've always hoped we might move back to Ontario. But *you've* always been happy *here*. Don't change the course of your career forever and ever just because it'll make me happy."

She rolled her eyes. "I love you, baby. More than my job, more than deep dish pizza, and definitely more than living in a metropolitan city. But I'm one-hundred-percent not suggesting we do this move *for you*."

"Bluewater Cove is everything you've ever wanted and more?" Skepticism dripped from his voice—and with good reason, she had to give him that even as she bit back frustration. Why did she have to spell out for him that everything had changed?

"Maybe it didn't used to be my top location pick, sure. But everything is different now."

"This sounds like nesting on an epic scale."

"Oh, really?" Laney swallowed back the louder-than-strictly-necessary snap that almost followed, because she could hear her mother still moving around.

"No?"

"No!"

He didn't say anything.

She sighed.

He laughed, just a little, with just enough of a rye twist that she knew he wasn't laughing *at* her. "Of all the things I thought we might fight about while you were pregnant, I honestly didn't see this one coming."

"What did you think we'd fight about?"

"You working too much."

She closed her eyes, squeezing them tight. He was honest to a fault with her. "I've been trying to be good about that."

"You've been *great* about that, babe. You're already a rock star mom. You've really..." He cleared his throat. "Changed. Oh. That's what you've been trying to say."

"Yeah." She rolled onto her side, her top leg pulling up against her belly. This was her favourite position to sleep in now. When she was at home, she spooned Kyle and Little Bean kicked him in the back. And then she'd roll over, and he'd follow, curling around her body and cupping the bottom curve of her growing belly with his hand. "I should have waited to tell you."

"You were excited. I'm sorry I dumped on your parade."

"I really am different now. Your kid has already messed with me on what I swear is a cellular level. I know you think this is just hormones, but I promise you, I know the difference between a temporary emotional outburst and my life priorities shifting permanently. I don't want to be so far from our family anymore. I wouldn't give up my career to be closer, but I would make different choices. I *want* to make some different choices. And this is a golden opportunity. If I don't take it, I'll be crying to you six months from now because I want to move home and I can't find a position anywhere. It's not like there are job openings for surgeons every day in small towns."

"I just want you to be sure this is a decision you'll be happy about two years down the road. Ten years. Once our kid is all grown up and heading off to Harvard like her mother."

Would she regret leaving the challenges and opportunity of a big city hospital behind? In the background behind Kyle, someone said something into his phone. She recognized his friend Willem. "Honey, I'll let you get back to your thing there. We can talk about this tomorrow."

"It's fine. These—" he broke off and swore good-naturedly at his friends. "These assholes just won't stop ribbing me for the lecture."

"I want to hear more about that."

"And I want to hear more about your crazy plan to move us, a dog, and a newborn to a whole new town and start over."

Shit. When he put it like that... she groaned. "Tomorrow, then. No decisions until I'm home, and we can talk about this seriously."

"In bed with some of Carrie's lemon squares?"

"Exactly. I'm picking up a double pan before I hit the road in the morning."

"I love you, sweetheart."

"I love you, too." She hung up the phone and pressed it to her chest. He was right. This wasn't a decision they could make impulsively or emotionally.

Against her hand, Little Bean rolled its head or butt or really giant foot from side to side.

I know, little one. I know.

5

———

The hour-long reprimand Kyle got from his advisor the next morning for his impromptu lecture to the undergraduate education students barely had any impact on him. Every bit of his worry was wrapped up in not being able to talk to his wife, who strongly preferred not to use her cell phone in the car, even on Bluetooth.

Whenever he looked at the clock, he instinctively pictured where she was on the familiar route from Wardham. By early afternoon, she'd be slicing across the top of Indiana. He wrapped up his office hour right on time —easy to do when your only visitor was another grad student wanting to procrastinate on their marking—and headed home, picking up the groceries to make an "I love you so much, I'm sorry we fought" dinner.

Since Laney had been a carb-hungry monster since getting knocked up, that meant oven-baked macaroni and cheese with cauliflower and a garden salad, heavy on the iceberg lettuce and fancy vinaigrette. And a loaf of Italian bread.

She was bringing home lemon squares, but he got a pint of vanilla ice cream just to be safe.

The pasta had just gone into the oven when he heard her car in the drive.

He met her at the door, but before he could say anything—"I'm sorry, I'm a dolt, we'll do whatever you want"—she was in his arms and kissing him.

"Hey," he finally managed to say when she came up for air.

She brushed her hair out of her eyes. The fine blonde strands had gone static in the long, dry car ride. "I'm going to convince you that moving is a good thing," she said firmly. "But first I want a shower and sex."

He grinned. Thank you, second trimester hormones. "We can do all three of those things."

"I don't want to be told I'm crazy and hormonal."

Oh, he wouldn't dare. Even when the hormones were to his advantage.

He peeled her out of her parka, then flipped the deadbolt while she greeted Buddy and gave him some love before sending him to the kitchen.

"Mommy and Daddy need to have some alone time," she crooned to their pup.

"Indeed we do." He tugged her upright and wrapped his arms around her from behind, his palms curving around her belly. Baby gave him a butt bump for being nice to the family VIP. "I'm sorry about yesterday. I didn't react appropriately."

"You reacted as you reacted. That part was fine." She took a deep breath. "Shower. I can't talk until I'm relaxed."

He grinned against her hair. He'd relax her, all right.

She laughed gently, shaking inside the circle of his arms. "Are you thinking about orgasms right now?"

"Of course."

With a sigh, she leaned back against him and tipped her head in. He found her mouth, soft and warm, and she twisted toward him again as he deepened the kiss.

"Show me," she whispered, leading him toward the stairs.

"Get naked, then."

She grinned as she slid out of her sweater. He unbuttoned his shirt. She wiggled out of her yoga pants. He lost his t-shirt. She stripped off her tank top, he shoved his jeans to the floor, and by the time they got to the shower, they were down to underwear. While the steam got going, they divested themselves of those last few scraps of clothing, pausing twice to kiss each other as the chemistry between them started to bubble.

They'd both made it a priority to protect the hot, sizzling hunger they still felt for each other. They'd been through a lot, and it was still just the start of their life together. They had a child on the way, a move in their future, and decades of fighting and making up ahead of them, and he always wanted to be able to give her this reminder of their connection, their primacy as a unit. They were partners in every way, and he'd slipped past worrying and wanting to protect her the night before into thinking he knew her heart and mind better than she did herself.

Limbs entwined, he washed her back as she rubbed her fingers up and down the line of hair running down his torso. He slowly turned her around, rocking his erection into her bottom as he stroked her belly, then lower, soaping between her legs. She was hot and slick for him already, but he wouldn't be rushed. He dropped to his knees and kissed their baby. He whispered how much he loved him or her, then he looked up at his wife.

"I love you, too, sweetheart. More and more every day."

Laney tried to tug him up to her, but he had a plan. She bit her lip, watching through hooded eyes as he nudged her back, leaning her against the tiled wall as he lifted one of her legs and draped it over his shoulder. He traced her folds with his fingers, dragging her slickness up to her clit before rolling that nub under his thumb. She immediately rocked her hips into his touch.

"You're so responsive," he murmured, and she mumbled something about *now* and *teasing*. He blew on her most sensitive parts in response. Her fingers tightened in his hair, tugging him closer. Smiling, he flattened his tongue and licked her slit, up and down, teasing at the top and swirling at the bottom until she was gasping for release.

Eager to give her that, he latched on to her clit and sucked, using his tongue to flick at the same time. Under his palms, her muscles tightened, then spasmed as she exploded into her first orgasm.

Her second came soon after he stood and slid inside her, holding her against the wall with his hands under her ass and his upper body pressed gently against hers. As she whispered a breathless stream of pleas in his ears, he surged hard, filling her over and over again until her heels dug into his ass and inside, her muscles started clenching again, milking his own release as he pressed deep one last time.

"I love you," he whispered as he lowered to the ground. "Here in Chicago. Back home in Wardham. Or wherever we end up. I'm right by your side for whatever adventure you want to go on next."

She cupped his face in her hands. Her eyes were steady and sure, even as her chest rose and fell unevenly. "I want to make Bluewater Cove our new home."

"Then that's where we'll go, my wife."

She squeezed him tight, and he closed his eyes, counting his blessings.

THE END (AGAIN)

WHAT TO READ NEXT

AN EXCERPT FROM WHERE THEIR HEARTS COLLIDE
(WARDHAM #3)

IT was a shame the guy next door was so rude. If he smiled, he'd probably be drop-dead gorgeous. If he smiled, that might mean she finally had his attention.

Karen peeked out the corner of her eye at the post-war bungalow on the other side of her driveway. The *shared* driveway. A mirror image of her house, with dark red brick and pretty white trim. A wide front porch—his was bare, except for a broom. Hers had her beloved bicycle in a place of honour, and a comfortable wicker conversation set decorated with navy cushions.

Between their houses sat his sensible four door sedan. Now it was awkward. *Should have told him the first time.*

She'd come home from work three weeks ago to find the house next to hers no longer vacant. Her standard welcome-to-the-street spiel had died on her lips as the new resident jogged out the door and straight past her, as if she hadn't been standing next to his front walk.

Technically on the sidewalk, but her intent to greet him had been clear. *Hadn't it?*

That was followed by two more non-meetings, which chafed her because she liked to be known as a friendly person. Forcing her neighbour to have a conversation crossed a line into needy. She'd been looking for a natural opening to a conversation. Now she needed to make it happen.

April was around the corner, and her Camaro was calling to be let loose on the road. As soon as the last threat of snow passed, she'd need to use the shared driveway to get 304 horsepower of Victory Red awesomeness onto the roads. Hard to do with his fuel-efficient safetymobile in the way.

So she was killing time in her front yard, pretending to tidy her flower beds, planning the best way to ambush a stranger. Not her finest moment.

Since he'd been home all day, he was probably going to leave soon. He worked shifts, leaving either early in the morning or around dinner time, and was often gone for the better part of a day.

She felt like a stalker, but really, he hadn't left her any choice. And it's not like she'd gone through his mail or trash. She really didn't know anything about him except for his schedule and where he parked. *And that he had single-handedly increased the hot quotient of Wardham by 1000%.* She didn't even know how old he was, although she guessed around her age, maybe a little bit older. No way would a guy in his twenties drive that car.

Two bags of twigs later, because pretending to work had turned into actually gardening, his front door opened. She stood, stretching her back before moving to intercept him before he could get to his car. "Hi! You must be my new neighbour." She offered her hand before remembering she was covered in dirt, and quickly converted the gesture to a wave. "Karen Miller."

He nodded, and stepped around her to put his duffle bag in the trunk.

"So, there was something I wanted to talk to you about, if you can spare a second?"

Another nod, and a raised eyebrow.

Karen paused a beat, then continued. "The driveway. It's actually a shared lane."

He glanced between their houses, then to his car, and finally back to her. He might not be big on words, but he wasn't shy about looking at her. He didn't seem shy at all, actually. She couldn't put her finger on it, but something about his appraisal seemed like a power play.

She bristled. "Look, your landlord should have explained this, and I'm sorry, but my car is in—"

"I bought it." His voice was quiet and calm, the opposite of his gaze. An unsettling combination.

"I'm sorry?"

"The house. I don't have a landlord."

"It wasn't for sale. I'd have seen a sign." It didn't matter, but something made her want to argue the point just because.

"Private sale."

"Well, okay, then your agent should have told you. It's a shared drive. My car is in the garage, and I'll need to—"

"My garage is full of junk."

So? "I need—"

"I'm busy until the weekend, but I can clear it out on Saturday. Sorry about the inconvenience." And with that, he turned to get into his car.

She knew she should let it go, but his quiet tone and half-listening had frayed her nerves. "You know, the interrupting is really rude."

———

Paul let his lips twitch slightly before he turned to face his feisty neighbour. He hadn't meant to be rude, but he could see how she'd interpret his words that way. "That wasn't my intention, I apologize." He leaned back against his car. He had a few minutes before he had to leave, and this might be fun. "I'm out of practice on being neighbourly."

She relaxed and slid her hands into the back pockets of her jeans, streaking dirt across her left hip. A curvy, round hip he had no business noticing, but she was right in front of him. With him slouched back against the car, they were almost the same height. He liked that she was tall. Too bad he wasn't interested in dating, or any other recreational activities, because there was a lot to like about this woman. Her sass, for one. Yeah, he really liked that. He grinned, and she rewarded him with a smile that bordered on sheepish.

"I'm sorry, too. You're obviously on your way somewhere, and I've just tossed this information at you."

"It's okay, I've got a minute. Why hasn't this come up before?" He knew that she walked or biked to work, although he hadn't figured out where that was. In a few more weeks, he'd probably know a lot more about her, and most of the other citizens of Wardham, but right now he was still commuting to the city.

"I don't drive much in the winter."

That explained the bicycle. Maybe she wasn't comfortable in the snow. "Do you have people who can pick you up when it's really cold?"

"What?" She wrinkled her brow, which was really cute, even for someone who was afraid of driving. Paul didn't usually have time for that kind of weakness, but he'd probably make an exception for his new neighbour. When a look of horror crossed her face, he realized belatedly that he probably wasn't going to get a chance to offer his assistance. "You think I'm afraid of snow? Or driving in general?"

Instead of being offended, she burst out in a beautiful peal of laughter that expanded until it encompassed him and he was chuckling along with her. "No? That's not...?"

"No." She smiled and leaned forward, as if to share a conspiratorial secret. "I drive a Camaro. It's my baby, and I have snow tires, but really, it's not built for winter driving."

Oh crap. Paul could see an entirely different encounter in their near future. Instead of offering to help with her errands, he was going to be writing her speeding tickets. "It's not?"

"Of course not. Some people love that thrill, rear-wheel drive, you know, but I'm all about the straight up speed. Dry road, warm summer day."

Damn. "Listen, Karen..."

"Yeah?" Her smile was wide and happy, and about to disappear.

"I need to finish introducing myself."

"Why? What are you, a cop or something?"

"Yes."

She blinked once, and twice, then her eyes got big and round and her hand slapped over her mouth. "Oh shit!"

He was about to apologize, for what he wasn't sure, when she started laughing again. He was quickly figuring out that she did that a lot. He liked it. Which was as good a reason as any to make his goodbyes and escape.

She breathed a contented sigh and stepped back, as if she sensed he needed to leave. He liked that too. "Okay, Constable. I look forward to sharing the driveway, and the roads around Wardham, with you, at a reasonable and posted speed."

His lips quirked and he nodded brusquely to cover

up. He had the funny feeling that Karen Miller could quickly get under his skin, and giving her any opening was just asking for trouble. Good trouble, but he wasn't in the market for that, or anything else. "Sounds good. I'll get the garage cleared out on the weekend."

He watched her saunter back up her front steps and lean over to collect gardening gear. His gaze lingered on her ass, until he forced himself to get in the car and drive away.

———

"There's a new sheriff in town."

Karen's best friend Carrie glanced up from behind the espresso machine. "Did we have an old sheriff?"

"You know what I mean."

"You have gossip about the new guy at the Wardham detachment?"

"Maybe. What do you know?" Karen slid onto a barstool. A Bun In The Oven didn't have tables, but three stools lived in front of the espresso bar for just these kinds of conversations.

Carrie laughed. "Not much, other than the position has been filled and the new person's going to start in a couple of weeks. He works in Windsor right now."

That would explain the weird hours. "The new person is Hot Neighbour."

"The rude guy?"

Karen shrugged. "He's a bit brusque, but I wouldn't say he's rude."

"You said he was rude yesterday. And twice last week."

"That was before I actually talked to him."

Carrie cocked an eyebrow.

"I stopped him today and asked him to start parking in his garage."

"Did you explain it was because of your *need for speed*?" Her friend giggled at the thought. It was true, though. In the summer, as often as she could find time, Karen headed out along the lake with the windows down. Alone with the wind and her music, it was hard to be 100% mindful of the speed limit.

"It came up. Before I knew he was a cop. It's not like I'm a criminal."

"No, but you like to drive fast enough that he'd need to pull you over. Of course, maybe that would be okay. Maybe he'd get you to step out of the car so he could frisk you."

"For a traffic stop? You've got issues." Although Karen couldn't deny that she'd enjoy being patted down by Paul. And interrogated. She shivered at the image of him leaning over a table at her, pinning her down with an inscrutable gaze.

Her friend pushed a latte and an orange cranberry biscotti across the bar. Fancy coffee still felt like a special treat in their sleepy little town. Karen grinned and dunked the hard biscuit. "Mmmmm. Oh my god, this is so good." She slurped a drip of coffee from her fingertips and waved off the previous conversation. "Do we have anything to discuss before the meeting tonight?"

Carrie nodded vigorously. "Oh yes! Apparently, the funding for the new community centre is going to be approved, so we should push for agreement on what the business association is going to lobby for in terms of sponsorship and space usage. I'd love to have a chance to bid for Bun to have a coffee bar there."

"Are you ready to expand already?" Karen knew that her friend loved running her coffee shop/bakery, but she knew from first-hand experience that being an owner/operator of a store was a huge endeavour. Bun had only been open for a bit more than year.

"The centre isn't going to open next week. It'll probably be a year or two before any plans need to be implemented. And there wouldn't be any food prep there, just drinks, muffins, scones, and the like."

"Hey, you know that I've got your back. Whatever support you need, you've got it." Karen took another sip of her latte. "Is there cinnamon in this?"

Carrie nodded. "Something new I'm trying. My own simple syrups. Less sweet than the commercial bottles."

"It's good." It had cooled down enough for bigger swallows now, and before long the mug was empty. "Was good. Now gone. Hmmm. Hulk happy."

"Hey, Hulk, before you go..." Carrie pinched her lips. Karen was surprised to see her friend look so uncertain all of a sudden.

"What?"

"The community centre. The draft plans that council saw last night feature a new library."

Karen shook her head. "That's great. Isn't it?"

"It is. But someone was there from the county library service, and she was talking about getting more involved in the community. Running book clubs, that kind of thing."

"Oh." She got it now.

"You could meet with her."

"And say what? Please don't offer a professional service that interferes with my hobby?" Karen shook her head. "I don't beg."

"Who says it needs to stay a hobby?"

If only that were an option. "I have a job, remember?"

"Yeah." Her friend dumped a heaping pile of understanding in that single syllable. More than anyone else, Carrie understood family obligations. "You could talk to your parents."

If only it were that easy. "They aren't the problem."

"You sell yourself short." It was a familiar argument. Karen had supported Carrie's dream of opening Bun, and Carrie wanted to return the favour. She couldn't wrap her head around the idea that Karen was happy with her life just as it was. It would be easier to convince her if Karen still believed that to be true herself.

"I gotta go to work. See you tonight?"

Carrie pursed her lips again and nodded. Karen had almost made it out the door before her friend called out.

"Hey, and don't think that's the last we've discussed of the sheriff!"

Karen laughed. As much as she'd like to fantasize otherwise, there was nothing to discuss. "Wardham doesn't have a sheriff, and I'm no librarian. Such is my lot in life."

KEEP READING WHERE THEIR HEARTS COLLIDE!

ABOUT THE AUTHOR

Zoe York lives in London, Ontario with her young family. She's currently chugging Americanos, wiping sticky fingers, and dreaming of heroes in and out of uniform.

Connect with Zoe:
www.zoeyork.com
zoeyorkwrites@gmail.com

BE A WARDHAM AMBASSADOR

I'd love to have you join my Facebook reader group!
Click on the link, or search "Wardham Ambassadors" on
Facebook.

https://www.facebook.com/
groups/WardhamAmbassadors/

9 781926 527819